How Many Blue Birds Flew Away?

a counting book with a difference

by
Paul Giganti, Jr.
pictures by
Donald Crews

Greenwillow Books, An Imprint of HarperCollins Publishers

For my mother
and father
—P.G.

For my boys Jack,
Gus, and Joshua, and
our friend Emma
—D.C.

How Many Blue Birds Flew Away?:
A Counting Book with a Difference
Text copyright © 2005 by Paul Giganti, Jr.
Illustrations copyright © 2005
by Donald Crews.
All rights reserved. Manufactured in China.
www.harperchildrens.com

Gouache paints were used for
the full-color art.
The text type is Futura.

Library of Congress
Cataloging-in-Publication Data

Giganti, Paul.
How many blue birds flew away?:
a counting book with a difference /
by Paul Giganti, Jr.; pictures by Donald Crews.
    p.   cm.
"Greenwillow Books."
Summary: Throughout the day, a child notices,
counts, and compares numbers of items,
such as how many boys and girls are on the
playground and how many more girls there
are than boys, until there is finally something
that cannot be counted.
ISBN 0-06-000762-1 (trade).
ISBN 0-06-000763-X (lib. bdg.)
[1. Subtraction—Fiction. 2. Counting.]
I. Crews, Donald, ill. II. Title.
PZ7.G364H1 2005 [E]—dc22
2004010868

First Edition 10 9 8 7 6 5 4 3 2 1

 Greenwillow Books

At breakfast
I took an apple
from a bowl of
apples and oranges
and I wondered:

**How many
apples
were there?**

**How many
oranges
were there?**

**How many
more apples
than oranges
were there?**

At the bus stop
I saw parents and kids
wearing hats and gloves
and I wondered:

**How many
gloves
were there?**

**How many hats
were there?**

**How many more
gloves than hats
were there?**

I looked up and
saw blue birds
and black birds flying
and I wondered:

**How many
blue birds
were there?**

**How many
black birds
were there?**

**How many more
blue birds
than black birds
were there?**

At school
I saw trucks
and cars parked
in the parking lot
and I wondered:

**How many
cars were
there?**

**How many
trucks were
there?**

**How many
more cars
than trucks
were there?**

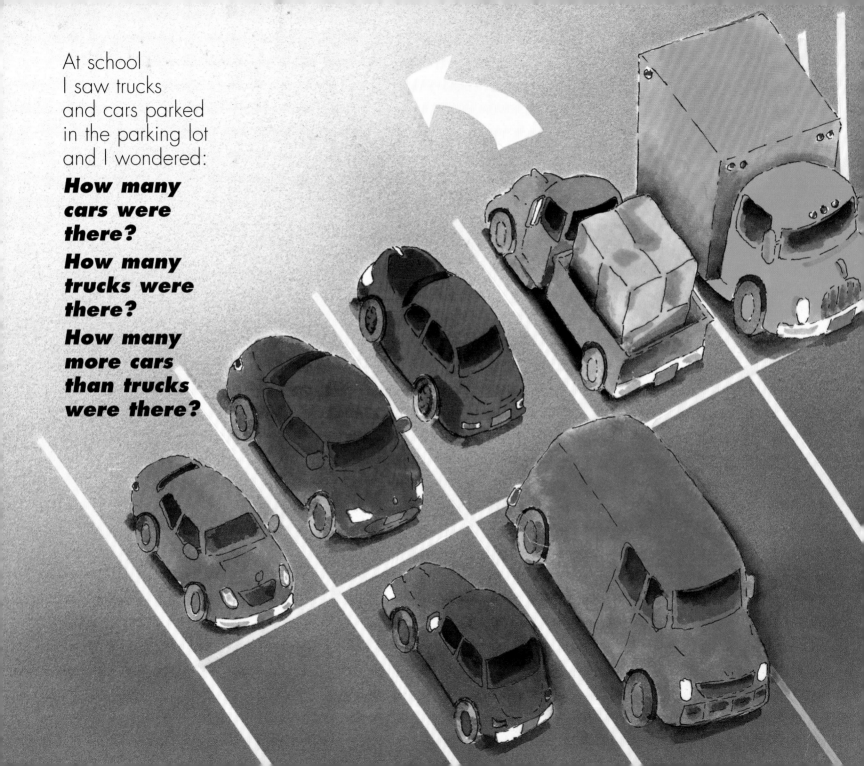

On the playground
I saw girls and boys
playing and
I wondered:

**How many
girls were
there?**

**How many
boys were
there?**

**How many
more girls
than boys
were there?**

On my way to class
I passed pictures
and classroom doors
and I wondered:

**How many
pictures
were there?**

**How many
classroom doors
were there?**

**How many more
pictures than
doors were
there?**

When I put
away my coat,
I saw coats
with buttons
and pockets and
I wondered:

**How many
buttons were
there?**

**How many
pockets were
there?**

**How many
more buttons
than pockets
were there?**

At my desk
I looked through
my pencils and pens
and I wondered:

**How many pencils
were there?**

**How many pens
were there?**

**How many
more pencils
than pens
were there?**

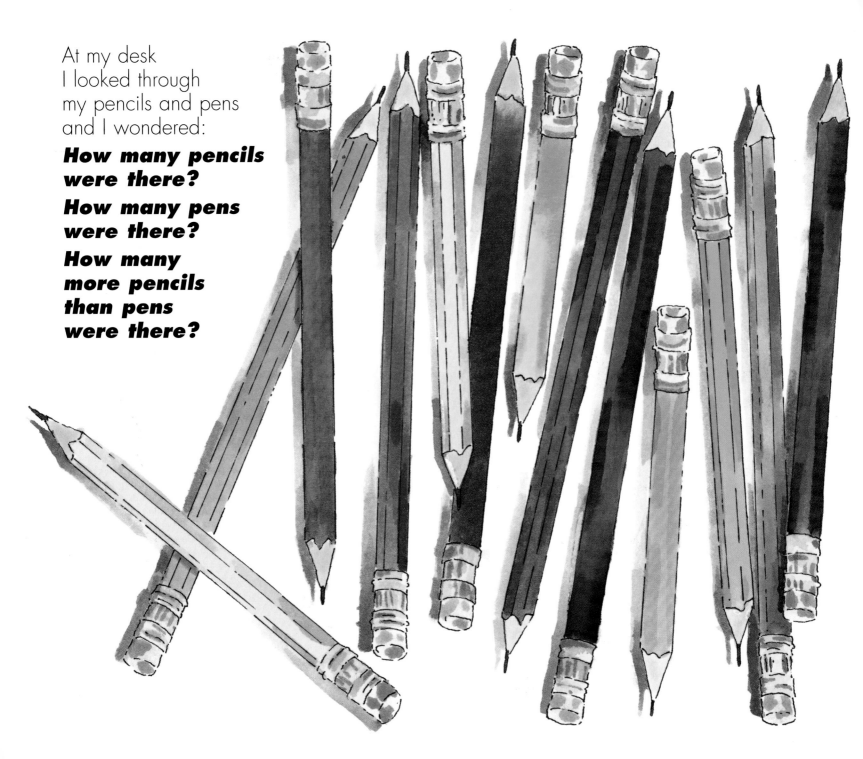

In our class's incubator
I saw eggs and chicks
and I wondered:

**How many eggs
were there?**

**How many chicks
were there?**

**How many more
eggs than chicks
were there?**

At lunch
I saw lunch bags and
lunch boxes
and I wondered:

**How many
lunch bags
were there?**

**How many
lunch boxes
were there?**

**How many
more lunch
bags than
lunch boxes
were there?**

When I was waiting
for the bus,
I saw flagpoles with
flags flying
and I wondered:

**How many flags
were there?**

**How many
flagpoles
were there?**

**How many
more flags than
flagpoles
were there?**

That night I saw the moon
and stars but I didn't wonder
how many more stars
there were than the moon
because there were
too many to count!